INTRINSIC

by

I0556292

Myriam Esthe

Published by
Myriam Esther Productions

myriamestherproductions.com

ISBN-13: 978-0-9903466-4-7

CHAPTER I

A myriad of black tulip umbrellas bloom with the first drizzles from the wonted cloudburst. Like ants in suits, they walk briskly undeterred towards their pre-determined goals outside bond street tube station in London.

Amid that restless zippy march, Fleur, a filthy motionless woman in rags in her mid-fifties, stands out like a sore thumb in the middle of the sidewalk. Nevertheless, she remains invisible to the crowd's furtive eyes in denial of what is deemed uncomfortable. Fleur looks twenty years older than her age, thanks to the 'natural street treatment' that carves deep wrinkles, making her look like the famous city of Pompeii. When she smiles, her sun colored teeth, shine while unforgettable gusts of alcohol slip pass her missing teeth. Fleur's attention seems exclusively focused on one young lady, entering the newspaper building holding a Starbucks coffee.

In front of the elevator, the young lady takes a tissue from her pocket and wraps her index finger with it before pressing the button. She keeps looking at her watch anxiously. Finally, her ride's doors open! Once solely confined in the closed up 'tin', she pops some Zanex pills before taking a sip of coffee. Her everlasting lift eventually lands on her floor. She frantically jerks out into an open office, rushes towards her cubicle, throws her coat on her seat before slouching in her chair. On her desk, there is a copy of a newspaper with her name and picture atop an interview with Prime Minister David Cameron.

Her boss Mike, resolutely plods toward her chomping on a sandwich seemingly held by sausage fingers. The noise of his chewing gets louder and the view of the shredded food resembling a trash truck grinder only magnifies as he gets closer. He hasn't swallowed half his food when he decides to vigorously attack his sandwich with one more massive bite before mumbling "That was a great interview with David Cameron, Claire!"

"Is it good enough to appoint me political editor?" Subtly moving her face away from those wafts of smelly food and spit sprinkles.

Mike's protruding abdomen is about to burst his shirt, as he bends down to put a big file on her desk "We shall see." Licking his fingers one by one "There are three others, contending for John's position. Show me a knock out article for the tenth anniversary edition and you might be a winner." Tapping the file on Claire's desk with his greasy bouncing index finger "Have a look at that file on the Conservative's proposed immigration law. I want an article on it for tonight's print."

"No problem, Mike."

Her boss finally walks away.

Claire grimaces as she stares in horror at the greasy fingerprints on the file's cover. She grabs a pen and uses it to flip the folder's jacket open.

In the evening, Fleur is still near the newspaper building sitting on the ground. She looks literally unwell, coughing non-stop and spitting blood. Some passersby flee away in disgust. She wipes her lips with her sleeve before asking them in a Spanish accent "Spare change, please?" Fleur coughs several more times, before hunching over a bottle of wine. She gulps down some of it, gets up teetering and burps before singing "You are the one, the one I love, you are the one, forever loved."
When Claire comes out of the newspaper building, Fleur stops warbling and gazes in awe.

The beggar keeps on peering at the young lady in motion, slowly disappearing down the stairs of the subway.

The following morning, Claire walks at a quick pace towards the newspaper building when Fleur staggers swiftly towards her shouting "Hannah!"

Claire carries on walking.

Winded, Fleur calls again "Hannah!"

Claire stops and looks over her shoulder.

Fleur looms closer.

The two women stare at each other. "I am not Hannah. My name is Claire."

Speechless, Fleur continues to stare at her with teary eyes.

"What do you want?" retorts Claire before turning her back walking away.

Tears brimming, Fleur begs "Please wait!"

Claire turns around "What do you want? I told you I am not Hannah!"

Fleur pauses with a peaceful smile on her face before noticing Claire's hints of impatience "Spare change, please?"

Claire's cell phone rings. She opens her bag to pick it up.

"Thank you!"

Claire looks confused realizing that Fleur thinks she's searching for alms. Annoyed, the young lady opens her wallet finding only a crumpled twenty pound note stained with red ink.

Fleur continues to stare at her.

The phone keeps ringing. Hesitantly, Claire fetches the note.

Fleur grabs Claire's hand and holds it tight before whispering "Thank you."

The two women stare at each other.

Claire's eyes are filled with repulsion and panic. She removes her hand from the beggar's grip and walks away. Her phone is still ringing, she picks it up with her left hand, lifting her right one, quarantining the contamination. Claire looks at her hand with aversion "Shit!"

Fleur in tears smells and kisses the twenty pound note gazing at Claire's silhouette in motion slowly fading away inside the newspaper building.

Claire rushes from the elevator to the restroom to wash her hand.

Mike intercepts and hands her a big file.

Claire takes hold of it with her left hand still lifting her right.

"Have a look at this file! What happened to your hand?"

"Oh! Nothing!"

Having no more hands to open the restroom door, Claire walks towards her desk and throws down the file.

Her co-worker Gerald's doltish head appears above the adjacent cubicle, pointing his finger to his watch grinning "It's nine thirty." He's a shlub, dressed in brightly colored and patterned clothes.

Claire stares at him with a grim smile.

Gerald's grin fades and he walks off to the coffee machine.

Claire walks back towards the restroom.

Mike hollers from a distance "Claire! I need the McPherson file! Send it over to me!"

Claire looks at her right hand and reluctantly retraces her footsteps.

Gerald puts a cup of coffee on her desk.

Claire shoots back at him a stare of annoyance.

"I thought you'd like one."

"Gerald, thanks but I only drink Starbucks!"

Disappointed, he retreats to his cubicle.

Claire types on her keyboard with her left hand to find the file requested. Whispering to herself "McPherson... Here you are!"

Suddenly, Gerald's head appears above the cubicle again, holding and displaying a printed picture of a clown with a caption saying 'smile.'

The picture startles Claire. Her brusque movements cause the coffee to spill on her leg.

At the sound of her shrieking sounds of pain, Gerald, still holding the picture, rushes towards her.

Claire briskly retreats.

"Sorry... I didn't mean to scare you. Are you okay?"

Claire is not responsive and seems lost in a day dream where she sees --Bright sun rays overshadow the face of a screaming, blood splattered clown, eyes popping out of his sockets.--

"Claire!"

The sound of her name brings her back to reality "Put that clown away, moron!" Claire inadvertently touches her cheek with her germ-contaminated hand trying to brush away a lock of hair in front of her eyes.

Horrified, she scampers to the restroom. She maniacally scrubs her right hand until it bleeds and splashes water on her face.

Completely drenched, Claire sits on the floor popping half the pills from her bottle to her mouth.

She looks dazed when Gerald comes in.

She quickly hides her pills "What the hell are you doing here?"

"I'm allowed in women's quarters, I was a eunuch in a past life."

Claire raises her eyebrows. She never has liked his weird sense of humor.

"But I'm fine now." Reaching for his fly "Do you want to check?"

Claire looks at him annoyed and lashes back sarcastically "Am I supposed to laugh now? Ha! Ha!"

Gerald kneels down to her level "Seriously, are you okay?"

"Yeah! I'm fine!"

"You don't look fine to me at all. You should go home. I'll speak to Mike."

Gerald helps Claire up when he sees a golden button on the floor and picks it up "Is it yours?" Looking at her outfit "It doesn't look like it."

Claire promptly snatches the golden button from him "It's my lucky charm. As a child I liked it so much that my father gave it to me. He used to carry it with him all the time."

As Claire waits on the platform for her train to come, she feels as if something has fallen on her head. She gently combs her hair with her hand. Her fingers are sticky. She nervously brings her palm forward to see what it is "Shit! Bird flu! Ah!"

Claire runs hysterically towards the exit inadvertently bumping into people blocking her way out. Once on the street, tears pour from her eyes as she rushes toward a small Victorian town house. She bangs hysterically at the door.

Sandra, a lively and eccentric black woman in her twenties, opens the door.
She wears a paint stained apron. She greets Claire with a huge smile on her face before asking her with a commoner accent "Hey! Hey! What's up girl?"

Claire pushes her way in. Sandra's place is filled with paintings. In the middle of the room, there is an unfinished painted canvas. Winded "You're the closest one to the tube exit... Sandra, it's horrible! I have shit on my head!"

Tapping her shoulder "I know girl, life is complicated."

Bursting into tears louder "No! Not that kind of shit! I'm going to die. I'm contaminated."

"By what?"

"Can't you understand? A bird shit on my head. I'm going to die. Bird flu. Oh my God!" rushing towards an open bathroom.

"Ha! Ha! Some say it brings luck!"

Claire comes out the shower wrapped in a bathrobe. With Sandra she doesn't hide the large surgical scar on her chest "Can I stay overnight? My parents are away for a wedding in Scotland and I don't want to be alone if any symptoms of bird flu appear."

"Of course! That's what best friends are for, protecting you against falling shit. Ha! Ha!... I'm worried about you. You don't seem happy."

"Why wouldn't I be? I have great parents, a good job, a loving boyfriend-"

"-So, even if everything is so great, you're still not happy? When I was a little girl, my parents had great hopes for me when we moved to the U.K. from Africa. They wanted a better life for me. They saved every single penny for me to become a doctor. My grandma noticed that I wasn't happy. She told me that everyone thought that being in London was a better life for her, but her dream, her inner need, was to look at the sea and nature from her hut in Africa. That was her true fulfilling happiness. She asked me then "What is your dream, Sandra?" I said "I want to paint." She convinced my parents to relieve me from their dream and allow me to study art instead of medicine. And I'm extremely happy today because I'm living my dream. Claire what is your dream?"

"To get the position as political editor."

"Bullshit! You're working as a journalist for a Labor newspaper just to piss off your conservative mom. A dream is no one else's or in spite of. It's inherent to your being. Without its fulfilment your soul is unbalanced."

Claire glimpses over at her cell phone expectantly "I don't know why James hasn't returned my call."

"You know perfectly well why! James only calls you when he needs one thing. You know he is no good for you. Ditch that douchebag!"

"I can't do that." Stroking her scar "No one else will have me."

Hugging her "You're beautiful. Plenty of fish out there who would love that scar because it's part of you."

Claire peeks at her phone disappointed.

"To take your mind off that jerk I have penis brittle for you... I mean peanut brittle, Ben and Jerry's ice-cream if you'd like?"

"Ah! Ah! Wicked!"

"Enjoy girl! There is some popcorn too!"

"Umm! Divine! You're the best Sandra"

Claire's cell phone suddenly rings. "James!" jumping to her cell phone to pick it up. Disappointed "Nope. It's mother." Opening her cell "Hi mom."

On the other side, Lady Martha Fioreli, elegantly dressed talks from a poshly decorated hotel room. She has an upper class British accent. Her husband, Sir Terrance Winchester, stands next to her. "Are you okay, sweetheart? I called your office and your boss Mike told me you took the afternoon off."

"Yes, everything is fine mom."

"I hope you are not filling yourself with ice-cream, hamburgers, and popcorn?"

Claire immediately wipes her mouth with her sleeve. With a swinging blow, she hits the popcorn tub sending it flying all over the floor "Of course, not!"

"Your father and I, are coming back from Scotland tomorrow. See you soon, darling. Here is your father."

"Love you, baby."

"Love you too dad."

CHAPTER II

Fleur peers through the building's front window. An elevator door opens with no one waiting, she rams her shopping cart through the front doors, past the security desk, and right into the elevator, which closes before anyone can stop her.

Everyone looks on speechless, at Fleur wheeling her cart full of junk; clutter toppling out as she goes.

Mike, exits his office with a file for Gerald. He looks at Fleur, but seems visually impaired by his own thoughts. He puts the documents on Gerald's desk.

Mike does a double-take and gives Fleur a disgusted look. Glancing at the ceiling "What is she doing here?"

"I need to speak to Claire Winchester."

Gerald takes the initiative to answer "Claire is not here."

"I have something for her."

No one in the office is eager to touch what Fleur has.

"Gerald! Take it!" orders Mike.

"Why me?"

Gerald reluctantly takes the wrapped gift and places it on Claire's desk.

With a chill in the night air the beggar, frantically coughing, sits on the sidewalk at her usual spot. With teary eyes, she kisses the photo of Claire on the editorial.

Before lying down, Fleur bundles herself in newspaper. She shakes and shivers as the rain sprinkles her face.

Struggling to breathe and with her last cough, blood runs from her nose and pours out of her trembling mouth.

She slowly slips from consciousness to visions of her earlier life.

--- A younger Fleur and Terrance, both in their twenties, come back from a costume party. Fleur in a princess dress and Terrance in a Victorian outfit, walk through Hyde Park each wearing a Venetian mask.

Terrance cuts off two buttons from his jacket and tenderly offers one to her. They are gold with a sapphire set in the center.

He puts the other button in his left shirt pocket "I've got you in the pocket of my heart, and when we get to America I'll marry you."

"Oh! Terrance."

They hug and kiss each other. ---

--- Fleur is about to give birth in a room above a cabaret. Pushing "Ah!"---

--- In an affluent section of Madrid, a seven year old Fleur, plays with her elder brother Jacob. She is dressed up as a princess and her sibling as a cowboy.

"When I grow up I want to go to Hollywood and become a star." shouts the little girl.

Jacob points his toy gun at Fleur who sticks out her tongue in response. She runs away and Jacob chases her around the room and grabs her.

"Stop it!"

"No, Fleur! You have to fight back. Let me show you what cowboys do to Indians."

Jacob's friend Aaron grabs Fleur's bangs "We should scalp her."

"Ha! Ha! Aaron, she is my sister."

"Brother, let's scalp him. He is the enemy."

Fleur is released. The sibling look at each other with accomplice smiles and start chasing Aaron.

Aaron now running "Jacob! You're my best friend."---

Fleur regains consciousness, looks for the 'cameras' and recites her last word "Hollywood." She closes her eyes embracing death with a big smile on her face.

CHAPTER III

The following morning, a horrified Claire finds a dirty cloth on her desk "What is that?"

Gerald's head appears above the cubicle "A hobo brought that for you yesterday afternoon."

Claire takes a pen to unfold the filthy fabric. A golden button is hidden within.

She takes from her pocket an identical button with her family initial engraved on it with a sapphire set in the middle.

She immediately rushes out to Fleur's usual spot next to the building shouting "Spare change!"

A policeman is passing by.

Claire approaches him. "Officer! Officer! Sorry to bother you, but, by any chance do you know where I can find 'Spare Change'? I mean the woman who was always begging over there?"

"Yeah! She is at the morgue."

"Oh, my God! Who was she?"

"Who knows."

Claire frantically looks up and down the street "Thank you, officer."

Bella, a homeless woman, clutches a bottle of wine.

Claire approaches her "Hi! I'm Claire Winchester. May I speak with you?"

Bella glances at her with a suspicious look. Slurring "Wa d'you wan?"

"To ask you some questions about the woman next to the newspaper building. What do you know about her? What was her name?"

"Maybe I know, maybe I don't. Depends on how much you have."

Claire fetches a five pound note from her purse.

She shows it to Bella, who grabs it instantaneously "Taco."

"Taco?"

"Ya! Are you deaf?"

"Do you find that funny? Give back my five pounds!"

"I ain't giving you back my fiver, baby! I nicknamed her like that because I have never seen someone eating so much Tacos! Everyone out here called her Taco, that was the name we gave her!"

"What was Taco's real name, before you came up with this incredibly innovative one?"

"Fleur, I think. I just know that before having the privilege of ending up on my turf, Taco was a singer at a place called 'Burlesque'."

Claire's cell rings. She thanks Bella before answering her phone "What's up Mike?"

"Where are you?"

"I'm investigating that homeless woman and-"

"-Who cares about an old tramp? Your job is to report on politics."

"But, Mike, it's-"

"-If you want that position as political editor, you better come up with a great story for the tenth anniversary. Have it for me by the end of the week, or the position will go to someone else!"

"Okay! I have a great lead on something politically smoking hot... And... I'm not going to the office this afternoon because... Because I have to interview my undercover... Mega huge big fish politician."

"Don't bullshit me! Who is he?"

Pretending "Hello! Hello! I can't hear you." Claire hangs up the phone and signals a taxi.

Arriving to the cabaret Burlesque. The door sign reads 'Closed.'

A young woman smokes a cigarette outside the back door. She wears a red leather mini skirt, with a plunging décolleté that showcase huge breasts.

Claire walks around the building and sees her extinguishing her cigarette on the ground with her high heel shoe. The young woman is about to go back in when Claire hollers "Hey! Wait!"

Claire runs towards her extending her hand "Hi! I'm Claire Winchester. Can I talk to you?"

The two women shake hands.

"Kathy. Sure, honey, you have five minutes before I go back in to rehearse for tonight's show."

"Do you know someone called Fleur, that possibly worked here a long time ago?"

Kathy stares at Claire, wondering "Do I know you?"

"No, I'm just trying to-"

"-You look familiar. Sorry, you say, Fleur? Fleur Larenza? She was an amazing singer. As a child, I used to be smitten when she sang with my mom."

"So, you knew her well?"

"Not me. My mom, Caroline, does. They were best friends. What's your business with Fleur anyway?"

"She passed away last night. Can I talk to your mother?"

"Come in! Mom's flat is on top of the cabaret."

"Thank you." Claire follows her.

"Wait here! Let me talk to her first."

"No problem."

Kathy comes back down "She's expecting you. You see that door on the right, give it a buzz love!"

Claire climbs up and rings the bell.

Caroline opens the door dragging herself around with the help of a cane "I'm Caroline. I'm glad you came. Please have a seat."

"I'm Claire. Thanks for having me on such a short notice."

Claire takes off her coat and sits in an armchair near the fireplace. Caroline tries to sit in another one opposite her. Groan "Owww!"

"May I help you, Caroline?"

"No, I'll manage, thank you. Ha! Ha! That's what happens when you try to do a split on stage at fifty-four."

"Wow!"

"The good news, I'll be able to do it better in a few months' time, with my new bionic hip replacement."

"Ha! Ha!"

Caroline reaches for a box from the coffee table. Tears roll down her cheeks "I can't believe that she is gone." She takes pictures out of the case and passes them to Claire "These are pictures of Fleur taken at Burlesque."

Claire gazes at one picture in particular "Fleur was stunning!"

Caroline shakes her head in despair "What a waste of talent! She so wanted to make it big in Hollywood."

"Did she go there?"

"Well, let me tell you her story..."

Claire is completely immersed into the tale. Through Caroline's words she's transported: Madrid in 1968, under dictator Franco's regime.

--- A convoy of military jeeps approaches. General Gonzales stares at a magnificent house. He orders his driver to stop with his ironlike arm. He then leaps out of the vehicle and knocks on the door with his brawny hairy fist.

Moshe opens the door "General, what deserves the honor of your visit?"

The General, pushes Moshe aside walking in with his bemired boots, tarnishing the impeccably polished floor. The General looks everywhere in ecstasy, like an entranced beast. To himself "What a beautiful house!"

Moshe's wife Debra, hugs her two startled children, Fleur, twelve, and Jacob, thirteen.

The General, takes the stairs to continue his tour of the upper floors. His eyes sparkle with excitement. To himself "Magnificent!" He rushes down the stairs and leaves Moshe's house with a smile on his face.

In the Evening, Moshe's family eat around the table. The Sabbath's meal is enlightened by two candles.

"Daddy, why was that soldier in our house?"

"I don't know, my sweet little Fleur."

"I don't like him. Let's go to Hollywood! I want to be in the movies."

"And I want to be a cowboy," proudly shouts Jacob.

Moshe smiles "Yeah! Let's all go to Hollywood for a while. Nothing good will come here, as long as Franco remains in power. Let's make my two little munchkins' dreams come true."

Fleur impatiently blurts "Can we go now?"

"Ha! Ha! Soon, Fleur, in a month when school ends. Let's sing!"

They all joyfully sing in Hebrew.
'*Shalom haleychem,*
Malachey hashareyt,
Malachey elyon,
Mimelech malachey hamlachim,
Hakadosh baruch hu.'

The following day, two military jeeps and an open truck full of prisoners stop in front of Moshe's house.

A crowd starts gathering around them.

Three armed soldiers enter the house.

The One-Eyed Soldier takes the stairs while the Fat Soldier grabs Moshe. The Bony Soldier seizes Debra's arm.

The One-Eyed Soldier comes back down pointing a rifle at Fleur and Jacob.

Moshe moves towards his kids "Fleur, Jacob."

Debra bursts into tears "Please, don't hurt my children."

The Fat Soldier hits Moshe's face with the butt of his rifle, while The Bony Soldier pushes Debra through the door.

Blood rolls down Moshe's forehead.

The Fat Soldier prods Moshe's back with the butt of his rifle "Communist bastard, move!"

"It's a mistake! I am not a communist!"

The Fat Soldier, hits Moshe in the stomach with his rifle to silence him "Fucking Reds!"

Moshe, Debra, Jacob and Fleur sit in the open military truck, among other prisoners.

A furious crowd throws tomatoes at the prisoners, shouting repetitively "Reds! Communist bastards!"

A chubby woman's head ventures out Moshe's adjoining house window, shouting "Swinish Jews. Burn in hell!"

A fountain of tears rolls down Debra's cheeks.

Moshe looks at them dolefully, while blood drips from his wounded forehead and forms a growing stain on his beige trousers.

Later that evening, General Gonzales, his wife Carmen and his children, eat joyfully around a table full of opulent food in Moshe's house.

In the meantime, Fleur's little fingers clasp the fence of an open-air prison camp. Her nose and lips protrude through the metal chain links. She gazes with envy at the birds' freedom. A tear rolls down Fleur's cheek as she whispers to herself "Hollywood."

Two soldiers bring out Debra and Moshe. They line the couple up against the prison factory wall and shoot them.

The sound of the gun shots snaps the little girl back to reality.

Five years later at Moshe's house in Madrid in 1973.

The General's wife is packing when her husband enters the bedroom "Come with us to visit my mother in Seville?"

"Carmen, I wish I could. I have some business at one of the camps outside Madrid."

General Gonzales gives a kiss and a hug to his wife before carrying the suitcase down to the car.

He stands on the stoop, waving goodbye to his family, who wave back at him. Their driver takes off.

In the evening, at the penitentiary camp in a suburb of Madrid. All the workers at the factory's prison look gaunt and filthy.

Jacob's face, now eighteen, is ravaged by a purple rash. Heavy drips of sweat roll down his face as he tries to assemble parts with great difficulty. His eyes shut sporadically.

Jacob starts shouting in delirium "Ha!" When Jacobs looks at his enslaved co-toilers around him, he sees them as vampires "Ah! Vampires are everywhere! Help me God!" Jacob grabs a tool and starts hitting his alleged vampires.

Two prisoners, one with black curly hair and one with glasses patched with tape, manage to pin Jacob down "Someone go and get Fleur!"

A mixture of cottage cheesy saliva and blood dribbles from Jacob's open mouth. Jacob is now completely unconscious.

"Jacob has typhus!" Shouts one of the workers.

The Glasses and the Curly Hair Prisoners, leap away from Jacob in panic.

A tearful Fleur, now seventeen, in prison rags, rushes to her semicomatose brother on the floor.

The Curly Hair Prisoner tries to prevent Fleur from advancing further.

She pushes him away and carries on moving forward. Fleur drops to her knees and embraces Jacob. She rests her brother's head on her laps, stroking his hair crying and screaming uncontrollably "No! No! Don't leave me. Please. Please! Jacob. Jacob, don't leave me alone!"

Jacob opens his eyes. He gazes at Fleur. A tear rolls down his cheek before his last breath.

Fleur screams frantically "No! Don't go! Ah! Come back, please. Come back. Come back."

An enraged Wooden-Legged Soldier, enters the factory walking unsteadily "Here you are bitch! Everyone is waiting for you!"

The Wooden-Legged Soldier stoops down, putting his weight on his good leg. He grabs Fleur's hair, lifting her face up from her dead brother. He drags Fleur out of the factory by her cowlick with staggering steps to the prison backstage entertainment room "Get changed bitch!"

Minutes later, Fleur makes her entrance on stage. Her face is painted with vulgar make-up. Bright red lips and cheeks with smoky eyes. Her French cancan costume, overly exposes her flesh.

In front of the stage, there are tables with drinking soldiers.

Fleur starts singing. A tear runs down the corner of her eye at the sight of General Gonzales drinking beer and laughing with three officers at a private table.

As the General gulps, foam clings to his lips looking at Fleur with desire, like a beast about to devour his prey.

The velvet curtain closes at the end of her act, prompting her to rush backstage, where The Wooden-Leg Soldier holds a pair of high heel shoes atop of a folded dress. He throws the lot at Fleur screaming "Put those clothes on, bitch! You're going away for a special weekend."

Before she knows what to think, Fleur is in the passenger seat next to General Gonzales in front of her childhood home.

The General takes out the keys from his pocket.

Fleur smiles as she stares at the cowboy key-ring her brother gave her father for his birthday.

She is violently awakened from her tender age memories when the General pushes her in the corridor.

Fleur looks briefly at the dining room. She closes her eyes to savor by recapturing in her memories the scent of the challah her mother used to bake.

The smell turns sour when the stench of swine sweat wafts her way as General Gonzales pushes her forward towards the stairs "Stop dreaming and move!"

Fleur looks at him defiantly and stands firm, stoically. She remembers her father telling her to never stop dreaming.

The General slaps her in the face. She falls on the stair "Get up, bitch!"

Fleur does not move.

The General grabs her by the hair and puts his gun on her temple "If you don't do exactly as I say, I will blow your stupid brains out."

Fleur gets up and carries on climbing the stairs.

Once in her parents' bedroom, General Gonzales gets undressed "Take your clothes off, bitch!"

Fleur reluctantly cooperates.

They both stand facing each other when the General pushes her head down.

The General's face filled with pleasure "Ah!"

The General's eyes look more and more distressed as he utters his last guttural grunt. He falls on his knees where his eyes level with Fleur's.

Blood drips down her mouth and teeth when in a victorious rage Fleur spits the General's penis in his face.

She pierces the General eyes still staring at her in horror with a simultaneous thrust of her two index fingers. His eyeballs pop out like popcorn.

The General tumbles to his back with each spasm of breath contorting his body.

Fleur picks up one of her heels. She impales the General's heart hammering the heel down to his chest with one blow of her fist. Blood spurts everywhere.

Fleur then draws the heel from the wound and throws away the shoe.

With her two bare hands, Fleur enlarges the wound tearing apart the flesh on the general's chest. She then plunges her two forearms into the open cavity uprooting the General's heart with her claws. She then throws it on the floor screaming in rage like a wild animal "Aaaah!"

The heart is on the floor, still beating .---

Claire is blown away by Caroline's story "Wow!"

"I'm tired and emotional, let's carry on tomorrow."

Claire looks at her watch "Oh no! I have to pick up my parents at the airport." Claire discretely wipes a tear "I wish I had talked to and hadn't judged Fleur while she was alive."

CHAPTER IV

Coming out of the arrivals' doors of Heathrow Airport, Lady Martha, exquisitely dressed, and Sir Terrance appear among the flow of passengers.

Claire and Terrance hug and kiss each other when Lady Martha breaks them apart pulling her daughter all for herself in her arms "It's so good to see you. I missed you."

"I missed you too, mummy."

Lady Martha, frowns as she looks at Claire's lips "My goodness! What on earth were you thinking with this reddish, 'hookerishtick' lipstick?" She takes a handkerchief out of her Chanel handbag and wipes her daughter's mouth with it.

They all walk to the airport garage and get into Claire's car.

Terrance is on the passenger seat next to his daughter while Lady Martha is in the back "Why did you stay at Sandra's?"

"Because I was not feeling well."

"Why didn't you stay at your friend Lisa's instead?"

"Why mom? Because she is white?"

"Hey girls! Don't start!" Begs Sir Terrance.

Undeterred, Lady Martha continues her argument "The polluted ideology of your left leaning newspaper, blows reason from your brain, bringing a plague of anarchy, rebellion, and disrespect for elders and traditions."

"Like the Thatcherist tradition of squashing the lower class?"

"I don't pretend to have a taste for politics but a woman with balls is quite admirable. A piece of art. Thatcher is quite a Picasso. But I do not appreciate the likes of Tony Blair removing my hunting rights!"

"What about animal rights?"

"There is nothing like shooting a rabbit or two... Hum! Fresh meat."

"Yuck!"

"Your loss, my dear vegetarian daughter."

Terrance smiles.

As soon as they arrive home, a maid greets them at the door and informs them that dinner is ready.

They all go to get changed.

Terrance, Lady Martha and Claire eat around a well-dressed table.

The maid enters with a bottle "Wine, Lady Martha?"

"Certainly, thank you."

"I'll have some too, please."

"Certainly, sir."

"And me too," joyfully says Claire lifting up her glass.

They all laugh.

Claire cell phone rings "May I leave the table, please?"

Lady Martha frowns "What cannot wait until after dinner?"

"Please."

Terrance smiles "Go ahead!"

"Thank you, dad."

Claire rushes out to the hallway.

Lady Martha rolls her eyes.

Claire grabs briskly her ringing phone lying on a low rise marble table in the hallway "James!"

"Hey! Baby cakes."

"I'm so glad to hear from you. But can I call you later? It's kind of a bad time right now."

"I'm outside your house. That's how you treat me?"

Claire peeks out the window.

A good looking playboy, is in a car parked in front of her house.

"But you should have at least called me to let me know."

"Am I not calling you now? Fine! You don't want to see me, fine I'll leave."

"No, wait! I'll come out in a minute." Claire hangs up the phone and rushes back to the dining room "I am terribly sorry; I need to go out. Something about work."

"We just came back. Can't you go at least after dinner?"

"No, sorry mom. I have to rush now. It's urgent."

"I can't believe it. Claire is so rude. Terrance say something!"

"Chill out, Martha." Smiling to his daughter "Go, Pumpkin!"

Claire rushes out of the room.

Terrance, still smiling, follows her.

Claire and Terrance are near the door when they hug and kiss each other.

"Thank you, dad. Love you. Bye!"

"Love you too, Pumpkin."

Claire rushes out.

After locking the door, her father pushes the curtain back slightly to peek through the window. He witnesses James kissing his daughter. He smiles before going back to the dining room.

James is in the driver seat while Claire is in the passenger.

"Are you taking me for dinner?"

"I've eaten already, and you are my dessert, baby cakes," frantically kissing Claire's neck.

Giggling "Stop! My parents will see us."

As soon as James enters his apartment, he kicks his shoes off his feet. Both his moccasins backflip landing on their soles. He pulls off his shirt and lets his pants fall off after he unbuttoned them like a pro with one hand. He punts his trousers with his foot 'scoring a goal' when the pants land on a chair nearby. His body bounces clear off the sheets from the propulsion of his kick. Moving his head like a cocky rooster, he taps his hand on the mattress to invite his bird.

Claire removes her dress slowly, giving her back to James. She hides the big scar on her chest with the frock on one of her hands while she stretches the other to turn off the light of the bedside table. She suddenly freezes her movement, thinking of Sandra's remark before turning around and uttering an insecure question "Shall I leave the light on?"

"I usually like it on... But yuck! It's kind of gross."

Claire blushes in humiliation.

"Sorry, I didn't mean to-"

"-That's okay." She turns off the light and lies down with a heavy heart next to James.

Like a beast, he doesn't waste any time and jumps on his cake savoring and enjoying his selfish dessert.

In the darkness, Claire can now quietly unlock the door to the painful flow of tears that were forcibly pushing to burst free.

Later on that night, half asleep, Lady Martha lifts her head and peeks at the clock which reads 2 a.m. She gets up and walks towards Claire's bedroom like a zombie, straining her eyes peering into the gloom to find an empty bed. She walks to the hallway, picks up the phone and starts dialing her daughter's number with no response. Worried, Lady Martha hangs up the phone and rushes back to her bedroom where Terrance's snores can be heard a mile away.

Tapping on her husband's shoulder "Terrance." The unresponsiveness of her spouse pushes her to shout more aggressively "Terrance! Wake up!"

Terrance makes a groaning sound. He moves to the other side of the bed, hiding his head under a pillow.

"Terrance!"

Mumbling "What?"

"Your daughter is still not home and she is not answering her phone."

From under the pillow "She is fine. Go back to bed."

Annoyed, Lady Martha unleashes a noisy spiel "Terrance, do something! With all those murderers, butcherers, caniballers... And God knows what else is at large outside."

Terrance uncovers his head from under the pillow making a weird face at the words her wife made up to rime "Butcherers and canibalers!?" Reluctantly getting out of bed "My dear, it looks like poetry was your forte at school."

He picks up his cell phone on the bedside table and walks out to his daughter's bedroom. He looks around before sitting on Claire desk's chair. He dials on his cell his daughter's number.

Claire sleeps and is unresponsive to her vibrating cell. Her phone carries on to quiver for few more minutes before she finally hears it and picks it up. Whispering "Dad?"

"Your mom was worried and made me call you."

"Sorry dad. I fell asleep and forgot to call you. Is mom mad at me?"

Unconsciously fidgeting with the two golden buttons on Claire's desk "It's okay Pumpkin. Go back to bed."

Terrance hangs up the phone and is completely flabbergasted when he finally notices the two buttons.

Lady Martha walks in and stops at Claire's bedroom entrance door "Did you managed to get hold of her?"

"Yes, she is fine. Go back to bed."

Leaving "Naughty girl!"

Terrance holds the two golden buttons in his hand pensively then suddenly rushes out of Claire's bedroom to his home office. He briskly opens a closet and picks up a big box that he lays on the floor. He opens it. Inside, there is an old Victorian jacket.

When he unfolds it, the attire reveals two missing buttons. Terrance kisses and hugs the jacket before bursting into tears.

CHAPTER V

The following morning Claire runs across the room towards her desk.

Mike juts out of his office eating a muffin "You're late! Any progress on the tenth anniversary article?"

"Working on it."

"I also need you to co-write with Gerald about B.P. gulf oil spill and Obama's response to it."

Claire glances at the clock on the wall which shows 12:00. She gets up and puts her coat on.

Gerald's head appears above the cubicle "Are you taking your lunch break?"

"Yep."

"Can I join you?"

Walking away, smiling "Nope."

Claire rushes out of the building. She stops and stares at Fleur's empty spot with a new feeling of nostalgia before resuming a brisk walk to fetch a taxi.

When she arrives at Caroline's, the two women embrace like old friends before Claire removes her coat "I'll have to be back at my office in an hour."

"Would you like something to eat?"

"No. Thank you Caroline."

They both sit down next to the fireplace.

At the sound of Caroline's voice recounting Fleur's story, Claire lets her imagination take her back to Spain 1973 where they left off.

--- Minutes after General Gonzales' death. Fleur takes a shower. The pure fresh water and the impure blood, merge and flux down her body to the drain. Fleur dries herself up. Wrapped in a towel she walks to the walk-in closet that she remembers so well. She used to like sneaking in to put on her mother's shoes which were always way too big for her tiny feet. She smiles with teary eyes before picking up some of Carmen's clothes. Once dressed, she searches General Gonzales' jacket on the floor and takes his cash.

Fleur spits on his eyeless face before permanently leaving her childhood home; this time on her own terms.

After running frantically in the streets of Madrid, Fleur lessens her pace before entering the train station. She looks at the departure times on the board.

A seventeen year old boy runs, threading his way through the crowd, checking his back incessantly with a frightened look when he inadvertently bumps into Fleur "Sorry!" The young man promptly grasps Fleur, precluding her from falling and quickly glances behind his back. In the reflex of the action, his bleeding right hand pops out of his pocket. He instantly hides it back in.

They both are bewildered when their pondering eyes meet.

"Aaron Stein?"

"Fleur Larenza? I heard you were taken prisoner."

"Shush!"

Aaron throws a furtive peek behind his shoulder.

Five armed soldiers zigzag in the crowd with furious inquisitive eyes, seemingly looking for someone.

As they come closer, Aaron embraces Fleur tightly and gives her a long kiss.

He unleashes Fleur as the soldiers safely outdistanced them "Where are you heading?"

"Hollywood. But I just want to get out of Spain first."

"There's a safe route from Morocco to America by boat. My uncle lives in Malaga. He can ferry us to Morocco with his fishing boat. It's only an hour away from there." Blood starts seeping through Aaron's outside pocket "We need to go."

"What did you do?"

"Not much really. Just barbecued some Francoists."

"Ha! Ha! The wannabe actor turned into an activist resistant. That role suits you better than the chicken in the Easter play."

Aaron playfully pushes Fleur away. "Where is Jacob? I miss that bastard!"

Fleur looks at him with tears slowly pouring from her eyes.

Large tears brimmed in Aaron's eyes in response.

They both walk in silence to the ticket office.

He is behind her in line.

Fleur's turn arrives. The ticket clerk signals for her to move forward "Where do you want to go?"

Aaron sneaks in next to Fleur answering in her place "Two tickets for Malaga, please."

"Thirty pesetas, sir."

Stepping back and pushing Fleur forward "My wife will take care of that."

Fleur reluctantly hands the money to the clerk.

She fires a frown at Aaron of disapproval.

Fleur grabs the two tickets and walks away.

Aaron catches up with her.

"I only have ten pesetas left now! You haven't changed! The same opportunist bastard!"

"I'm sorry. I'm broke. I haven't eaten for two days."

Fleur's facial expressions loosen up. She gives him his ticket.

They have been on the train for an hour now.

Aaron slumbers with his head against the train's window.

Fleur comes back to her seat "I got you some food."

Roused from a deep sleep, Aaron yawns "Thank you." Glancing at his watch "We should be in Malaga in two hours."

Once in Malaga, Fleur and Aaron walk to the port where a fisherman waits for them.

"Hey! Uncle Samuel. How are you?" They hug and kiss.

"So good to see you. Who is she?"

"Don't worry, uncle. Fleur is a friend of mine."

"Let's go before anyone sees us!"

Samuel pilots his boat while Aaron smokes a cigarette.

Fleur rapidly falls asleep on the deck, near some opened fish tanks.

At dawn, they reach the port of Tangier in Morocco.

Fleur and Aaron wave goodbye to Samuel.

Wiping a tear "My uncle looks so much like my late father. I hate those Francoists!"

Fleur puts her hand on his shoulder to calm him down.

"My uncle said that we need to find a ship called 'Salah'. It regularly goes to America transporting olive oil."

"How are we going to pay?"

"I don't know. Maybe the captain will take us on board in exchange of some chores."

They scout the port checking the name of every boat's bow when suddenly Aaron shouts "Look! Salah."

The captain of the boat comes out of the ship with three other men.

"Stay here! I'm going to have a word with the captain."

In the meantime, Samir a bearded man in his fifties, dressed in a white tunic and a turban around his head, passes by Fleur holding five camels on a leash.

"El ben jamilah."

"What?"

"Al anat metorzowish?"

"Sorry. I don't understand Arabic."

Aaron runs back to Fleur interrupting her conversation with Samir.

"It's no good. The captain wants five hundred dirhams per head."

"What are we going to do?"

"I don't know."

"When is the ship leaving?"

"In two days."

Aaron and Fleur walk on the beach.

Fleur takes a big breath in, "It's beautiful."

Samir walks on the beach with his camels and approaches them again.

"Malchabra!"

"Malchabra!"

"Aaron, I didn't know you speak Arabic."

"Yoom kinei etarat dofma aka?"

Aaron nods his head. "Fleur, wait for me here!" Heading towards Samir.

Aaron and Samir walk away together before ensconcing themselves from the frying sun rays under the leaves of a gigantic palm tree.

Fleur dips her bare feet in the sea while a slight breeze ruffles her hair, uncovering two wondering eyes focusing on the two men.

Aaron walks back toward Fleur holding three camels on a leash.

Fleur lets escape a roar "Ha! Ha! What are you doing with those camels?"

"Listen! Everything is under control. I'm going to sell those beasts at the market. We should get a good price for them. Enough for our tickets."

"I don't understand. How did you pay for them?"

Aaron looks away "They were free."

"Why did he do that? We don't even know the guy."

Aaron reaches up and tousles his hair "Moroccan hospitality, I suppose." Walking away, pulling the camels.

Fleur follows him.

Aaron turns his head around "Listen! It's better you go with Samir. His wife is going to feed you and you can freshen up. I'll join you later."

"You want me to go with him? I don't even understand him."

"Trust me!"

Samir brings another camel for Fleur to ride.

"Let me help you up!"

Bewildered, Fleur lets Aaron launch her to the camel's back.

The camel briskly gets up to the sound of Arabic words.

Fleur sways. She holds on to the beast as tight as she can.

The Bedouin moves away pulling her camel on a rope.

"Aaron."

Aaron moves away in the other direction ignoring Fleur's call.

After an hour of going through infinite dunes of sand, the flashes of sun rays give the illusion of a blazing horizon, where the vague silhouettes of white tents and camels peak over shimmering.

Fleur and Samir finally arrive at the Bedouin camp consisting of a scattering of modest tents with a conspicuous giant white one at the center. The crowded oasis throbs with life.

As Fleur approaches on camel the Bedouins stare at her. Very quickly the noise decrescendos to a complete silence.

Samir helps her down off her camel.

Fleur follows him to the giant tent. She is flabbergasted by the lavish interior and the opulence of the food lying on golden dishes "Wow!"

"Kalkela!" Samir makes a gesture bringing his hand to his mouth for Fleur to grasp the meaning of his words, before he retires.

Fleur smiles, bouncing on the tip of her toes towards the grapes. She joyfully starts devouring them like a glutton. She cheerfully pirouettes when a young girl dressed in a traditional Arabic outfit silently slithers in.

"Oh! Sorry. I am Fleur. What's your name?"

"Saturday."

Fleur and Saturday smile at each other.

In the evening, Fleur sits in front of a mirror wearing a beautiful Middle Eastern dress, while Saturday brushes Fleur's hair.

Outside, the indigenous dance around a bonfire to the sound of drums and tambourines, while women ululate, flapping their tongues on the roof of their mouth creating a continuous high-pitched tone.

Karim, the chubby and short sheik of the Bedouins' tribe, sits on an elevated Persian mat surrounded by five women.

When Fleur shows up at the gathering with Saturday, Karim's eyes follow Fleur like magnets.

Karim waves his hand to summon them near him.

The two young girls oblige giggling.

Fleur sits next to him.

He communicates with her in English "I'm Sheik Karim. You're beautiful."

"Thank you."

"You are Sunday."

"No. I am Fleur."

"No! You are my beautiful Sunday. Okay?"

Fleur's body shakes with mirth as she stifles a giggle "Okay."

Karim gestures to the six women surrounding him including Saturday to go dancing.

The six women dance with ceaseless moves, swinging, twisting, dropping their hips and their pelvic with perky foot and leg work.

Their bodies shimmy and undulate like a storm-tossed sea.

Karim smiles and claps his hands in an effervescence of high spirits and exultation "My wives are good dancers?"

"They are all your wives?"

"Yes! I have six wives." Pointing each of them "This one is Monday, this is Tuesday, Wednesday, Thursday, Friday, Saturday and you-"

Fleur's jaw drops while her eyes flip in horror "-No!"

Karim crawls over Fleur "You are my beautiful Sunday." Putting his hands all over her.

Fleur pushes them away and stands up "I cannot be Sunday!"

"Why? You prefer another day? Don't worry! Once you got your slot in, you can swap with the others."

"Ah! No!"

"So, you are Sunday."

"I cannot be any day, because... I'm fully booked all days of the week... for life, with, with... My husband Aaron. He should be here soon. He is very, very jealous."

"Jealous? He sold you to my servant Samir for three Camels. You are mine now!"

Fleur's face oscillates from decomposing slowly as she realizes the truth to quickly gathering steam before exploding into a rage "Ah! Three camels! Opportunist bastard! He sold me for only three camels?"

"I know. You are worth much more."

Fleur grabs some oranges and pelts Karim with it.

Karim ducks to avoid them "They were good camels though."

Fleur hurls a plate. It misses him by little "Ah! Three camels!" Fleur hunts down Karim, hurling anything she finds on her way at him.

Karim shelters inside the big white tent. Panting "Calm down! I will give him ten camels."

"No! Don't give the bastard any more camels!"

Karim quickly girds his arms tightly around Fleur and pins her down on the bed. He smothers Fleur with kisses.

"Get off me! Look! You can't do it!"

"Why? You are mine, I can do what I want."

"We are Saturday today!"

"Oh! Really? Well, that's okay, I can have two days in one." Karim carries on kissing her.

Fleur pushes him away "I refuse! I am Sunday. The shop is closed today!"

Bewildered "Hum! Fine then!"

Two armed Bedouins guard the tent where Fleur spends the night.

The following morning, the two armed Bedouins walk abreast, leading Fleur to the big white tent.

Karim sprays perfume all over his body. He then polishes his teeth with mint leaves. He chews and spits the foliage, as Fleur is forcibly delivered to him by the two armed Bedouins who swiftly retire.

Fleur twists her mouth in disgust.

"Here you are my beautiful Sunday!" Karim jumps at Fleur with excitement.

"Wait! Isn't it a bank holiday today?"

"Oh! Yeah baby! It's a bonk holiday."

Karim grabs and kisses Fleur.

She struggles to free herself and bites him.

"Ha! Ha! You like it rough. Okay then." Karim grabs a whip and lashes the floor with it.

Fleur runs in fright "Ah!" She trips over something on the ground.

Karim jumps on the top of her.

"Ah!"

"I got you."

Karim upper body falls smothering Fleur.

Buried under Karim's inert body "Hey!"

Karim is unresponsive.

Fleur tosses away his body and emerges from underneath perplexed.

Karim is motionless on the ground.

Fleur listens to his heart "Oh my God! No!" She gets up and grabs a blanket wrapping herself from head to toes in it before getting out the tent.

She tiptoes to a camel on the outskirts of the oasis and climbs on it "Come on get up!"

The camel is unresponsive.

"Come on!"

The camel is still sluggish.

"I'm going to slap you in the butt if you-"

The camel turns his head around and spits at Fleur.

Fleur wipes her face with her hand "Yuck! That's it!" She turns around riding the camel backwards and bites his butt.

The camel rises and springs with Fleur on his back facing backwards.

"Ah!"

Fleur is on the back of the camel. She turns around to ride it face forward.

The camel halts.

Fleur alters to ride it backwards again.

The camel carries on trotting briskly.

She had been riding for a while when suddenly, a biplane flying over her, loses control and heads towards her.

Fleur sees the plane but the camel doesn't, as he faces the other direction. To the camel "Ah! Move away!"

The biplane grazes Fleur's head before the pilot manages to land the smoking, crippled plane several yards away.

In the fright of the moment, the camel lurches, hurling Fleur into the sand.

A disgruntled Fleur lifts up her embedded head.

The camel plops down a few yards away apathetically.

The pilot survives the plane crash with only few scratches. He leaps out the smoking plane.

As he walks towards Fleur, the plane explodes propelling him a short distance.

Fleur and the pilot face each other lying on their stomachs and lifting up their heads simultaneously like turtles.

"Hi! I'm Terrance."

"What's wrong with you? You almost decapitated me. You had the entire desert but no, you had to land precisely where I am!"

"Sorry. Fatal attraction I suppose. Do you always have this magnetic effect on men?"

Fleur's body shakes with mirth as she stifles a giggle with an overwhelming tug of attraction in her eyes.

Later on, the camel sits on the sand with Terrance on his back "Come on! Climb!"

"He is not going to move. You have to ride him backwards."

"Nonsense! Come on!"

Fleur climbs on the camel.

To the camel "Go!"

The camel remains still.

"I told you. Let's flip around."

"Why would he move only ridden backward?"

"Because he is scared we will bite his butt."

"Why would the camel think that?"

Fleur's face is illuminated by a smirk.

Terrance, realizing, begins to laugh. He holds Fleur in his arms while riding backwards the camel in motion.

A sand storm emerges.

Terrance and Fleur approach a Bedouin village.

"The sand storm is getting more perilous. Let's spend the night here!" Suggests Terrance.

They both get off the camel.

The curious Bedouins approach them.

Terrance takes his watch from his wrist and offers it to the Bedouin chief. He gestures his words for the indigenous to grasp the meanings "Hi! Can we have some food and a place to sleep overnight, please?"

The Bedouin chief nods.

Terrance and Fleur sleep back to back on the ground next to each other in a small tent.

They turn serendipitously toward one another.

They mirror a smile while Terrance brushes gently with his fingers a lock of Fleur's hair from her eyes.

Terrance moves forward and lays his lips upon Fleur's. The kiss gradually intensifies into devouring passion.

They tactfully undress one another before laying entwined in each other's arm copulating passionately reaching a reciprocal pleasure expressed in their faces.

Terrance and Fleur sit on the floor looking at each other with their legs entwined.

Stroking her head "Why do you want to go to Hollywood?"

"I lost everything I love. My dream is the only thing I still have. The only drive that keeps me alive. I'd like to be like Marilyn Monroe."

"I believe you can make it. I can help you if you'd like. Come back with me to London and I'll see what I can do for you with my connections in Hollywood."

"Really?"

"Yeah! I have my family fortune to manage and I think you are a good investment. Such a good looking investment!"

They both laugh as Terrance kisses her.

In the morning, Terrance and Fleur are on the back of the camel but this time they ride it forward "Hut-hut."

The camel moves straight.

Terrance and Fleur laugh simultaneously.

"Gee!"

The camel turns right.

"Haw!"

The camel turns left.

Terrance and Fleur giggle and kiss each other.

"You are a natural riding camels, better than with planes."

"Thanks to the Bedouin instructions."

Later, Terrance and Fleur kiss in front of a bank in Tangier.

"I don't want to scare you away but I think I love you."

Fleur kisses Terrance in response.

"Wait for me here! I'm going inside to change some sterling pounds into dirham."

Fleur stands outside when two policemen handcuff and take her away.

When Terrance comes out of the bank, he is surprised not to find her.

He looks for Fleur everywhere screaming her name in vain. His steps crescendos in harmony with his worried facial expressions "Fleur!... Fleur!"

The sound of Terrance's voice is suffocatingly ingested by the noisy crowd.

In the meantime, being held captive in a prison, Fleur grips the bars of her cell, her nose and lips protruding. A tear rolls down her cheek as she closes her eyes mumbling "Hollywood."---

Claire wipes a tear "Poor Fleur."

Caroline sighs "Fleur spent ten years in a Moroccan prison. She escaped the death penalty because sheik Karim had died of a heart attack."

"So why was she sent to prison if he died of a natural cause?"

"Well, the judge ruled that she was indirectly guilty for triggering it."

"What happened when she was released?"

"Fleur took a boat to England to look for Terrance."

Claire once again let's herself transport by the flow of Caroline's words to Fleur's life story.

--- Fleur now twenty-seven is aboard a cargo ship. She is on the deck gazing at the roiled sea. The whistling wind blows, churning and vigorously clashing the waves. Her hair floats in the air. She closes her eyes. Her facial expressions are flooded with swirling emotions as she inhales the salty smell of the sea.

Weeks later, when she finally disembarks in the port of Liverpool, she hitchhikes her way toward the capitol where the love of her life is to be found. She had dreamt of this moment for ten years in her gloomy cell.

When she finally reaches London, Fleur walks in the streets looking for a phone booth. When she finally finds one, her hands shake as she opens the yellow pages. She impatiently runs through the pages with her index finger through names with excitement. She can feel the hastening of her heartbeats as the adrenaline flows through her veins like the rapids. Fleur feels her heart falling to her feet when her finger finally stumbles on the name of "Sir Terrance Winchester". She scribbles in disbelief on a piece of paper Terrance's address and phone number with a shaky hand. She keeps kissing the note overwhelmed with joy.

CHAPTER VI

Terrance, Lady Martha and their respective fathers, Sir Winchester Senior and Sir Rocco Fioreli, are at a polo match.

Terrance and Lady Martha sit next to each other while their fathers have the seats behind them.

In a robotic reflex, Terrance's arms synchronously rise with those of the audience to the stimulus of a goal "Yeah!"

Lady Martha laughs.

He stoops back in his seat with a giant congeal smile.

Lady Martha hugs and kisses him.

The mirroring smiles of their fathers, bestowed a loving seal of approval.

Lady Martha turns around "Your team is doing really well, papa!"

"Thank you, darling."

"You missed that investment, dad!" Adds Terrance to his own father.

"Son, Rocco is always one game ahead of me."

Unanimous laughter.

They all celebrate Sir Rocco Fioreli's team victory at Terrance's home.

The host opens a bottle of champagne and joyfully pours it into crystal flutes. Lifting one up "To Sir Rocco's polo team!"

They all happily drink.

Fleur, stoic outside, feels a sudden overwhelming flow of emotions rushing from the bottom of her heart to the tip of her rusty fingers. Her right hand moves frantically back and forth, with her eyes following the small piece of paper. The repetitive oscillation makes her dizzy. Certain but still in disbelief that it is Terrance's house, she gathers the courage to bring her little trembling hand to push the conspicuous door bell.

A maid opens the door.

Fleur is speechless. How could it be? She has been rehearsing that moment for ten years. She tries to choose the right words among a myriad that clutter her brain all at once "Hi. I am looking for Terrance Winchester, please."

"Does Sir Terrance know you're coming, madam?"

"No. But I am... was an old friend of his."

"Please, come in."

"Who may I announce, madam?"

Pause. She forgot her own name when suddenly her lips mechanically utter, "Fleur Larenza."

Fleur waits in the hallway while the servant goes to fetch her master. All of a sudden, one of her legs starts shaking uncontrollably. She tries to stop it by holding it tight with her two hands but nothing seems to work. To help herself calm down, Fleur looks at the beautiful paintings on the walls. Dripping with sweat, Fleur realizes it's more than she can bear. She resolves to leave but her other leg has decided to quiver in chorus with the other one.

"Is it really you?" Questions Terrance to Fleur's back.

Inexplicably, both her legs stop shuddering at the sound of his soothing voice. She slowly turns around.

Their sparkling eyes immediately find their target, staring at each other with flickering embers.

"Oh my God! I thought I lost you. I looked for you. I thought-"

Fleur places a finger before Terrance's pursed lips to hush him.

"Where were you?"

"It's a long story. I was held captive against my will."

"Why you didn't tell me?"

Fleur looks down and starts crying.

Holding her in his arms "That's okay. I'm sorry."

Lady Martha's voice "Terrance."

Terrance signals Fleur to remain silent. He then pushes her in his office and briskly shuts the door.

Lady Martha enters the hallway "Here you are!" Giving him a kiss "Dad and I are going back home. Thank you so much for coming with me to the match and for the party."

"You're welcome."

"Can I see you tomorrow?"

"Hey! Take it easy. I thought you agreed we're just friends."

Winking "With benefits."

Sir Rocco Fioreli approaches them.

"Thank you, Terrance. You definitely are a good catch!"

Terrance forces a smile holding the door while Lady Martha and her father walk out.

In Terrance's office, Fleur peeks through the window. She suddenly realizes that during all those years in her delusional, romantic scenario, she has never thought of the possibility of Terrance being with someone else. She feels overwhelmed by shame and embarrassment as he enters the room and grabs her hand.

"So you're in town and decided to say hi. Nice to see you."

Fleur looks down "Yeah!"

"Let me know where you're staying. I'll give you a call sometimes this week and we can catch up. I've some business to sort out with my father."

Eyes brimming "I shall leave now then!"

Fleur moves toward the door when Terrance holds her back by her arm "Did I say something wrong?"

Bursting into tears "No."

"I don't understand. We made out once briefly a decade ago. What do you expect?"

"Nothing." Fleur opens the door and rushes out.

Terrance let her go. ---

"He let her go just like that?" Asked Claire.

"Yeah! Just like that!... He stood there on the door step following her with his eyes until she disappeared past a building across the street." Replied Caroline.

"And then what?"

"He ran as fast as he could to catch up with her and the rest is history."

"For real?"

"Yep! For real. The chemistry between those two was out of this world. They were true soulmates."

"I want to know everything."

"She moved in with him. They were inseparable. He unrolled her in 'Lambda,' one of the best acting schools in London. He lavished her with clothes, jewelry and so much more... Then two months later..."

Claire is again transported through time by Caroline's words.

--- Terrance and Fleur come back from a costume party. Fleur wears a princess dress and Terrance a Victorian outfit. They walk through Hyde Park with Venetian masks covering their faces.

"The party was really fun," says Fleur.

"The Lambda director told me you're ready. You could make it big here in the U.K. if you'd like. Are you sure you still want to go to Hollywood?"

"Yes."

"Fine then. I'm coming with you."

"Are you serious?"

"Dead serious. As a matter of fact-" Terrance cuts off two golden buttons from his jacket and gives one to Fleur. "-This Jacket has been given to my ancestor by Queen Victoria. It had been specially tailored for him with pure gold buttons encrusted with unique sapphires with our family initial engraved. It's my favorite possession. Please take this button as a token of our love. When you look at it, always remember how much I love you."

Fleur takes the button. They both hug and kiss each other.

She kisses the other golden button in Terrance's hand before he puts it in his left shirt pocket. "I've got you in the pocket in my heart, and when we are in America I'll marry you." ---

"No way! Dad was about to marry Fleur? But what happened?" Interrupts Claire."

"Your mother Martha came to pay him a visit." Replies Caroline.

--- "I heard you are eclipsing away to America like a thief with that commoner."

"Martha, don't talk like that. What I do is none of your business."

"I love you, Terrance."

"I'm sorry. You and I were never together. It was just a fling and you knew that perfectly well. I'm going to marry Fleur."

"No, you are not!"

"Please don't make it more difficult."

"I'm pregnant."

Terrance holds his head with his hands in despair, pondering his answer, "I'll stand up to my responsibility, but I'm still going to America with Fleur."

That evening, Terrance closes his suitcase. The bell rings. He opens the door, his father, Sir Winchester, stands on the stoop.

"Hi! Son. I was just about to buzz again. Can I talk to you for a minute?"

"Dad! I don't have much time, the cruise ship to America is leaving soon."

"A cruise ship! Boy you are spoiling this outcast girl."

"Please dad. Don't talk about Fleur like that. I want her to see Hawaii. Our last stop will be Los Angeles where we'll be living."

"Sorry. There is a problem son. You cannot go. Martha's father told me that he will ruin me if you dishonor his daughter."

In the meantime, Fleur looks at her watch anxiously.

Passengers stroll by her, boarding the cruise ship.

Fleur still waits, looking at her watch nervously.

The captain stares at her from the departure gate before walking towards her, "Madam!"

Fleur turns around.

"You should board the ship now; we are leaving in fifteen minutes."

Large tears brim in Fleur's eyes. "Please, a few more minutes?"

The captain purses his lips tossing his head and walks back to the departure gate.

A black luxury car stops in front of Fleur. The driver gets out the car, "Fleur Larenza?"

"Yes."

"I've something for you." The driver gives her a big envelop.

Fleur opens it briskly. In it, there is a lot of cash with a handwritten note. She reads it with her face flooded in tears. '*Fleur, sorry I misled you but I'm not coming with you to America. It was a foolish idea. Please don't ever try to contact me or see me. I'm going to marry Martha; the woman I love. I hope the money will help you in your endeavor. Sir Terrance Winchester.*' After reading the note, she faints.

Paramedics arrive to her rescue.

Fleur lies on a hospital bed when she opens her eyes.

The nurse standing next to her puts a damp cloth on her forehead. She senses fear in Fleur's eyes "Don't worry! You're just fine."

"Why am I here? What's wrong with me?"

"You fainted and bruised your head. The good news is you are still pregnant. The bad news is you missed your boat and can't travel in your condition. There are complications with your pregnancy. You must rest!"

"Pregnant? We missed the boat?" ---

"Wow! Unbelievable! I have a half sibling?" Interrupts Claire.

"Wait! Don't get too excited!" Replies Caroline before resuming her story.

--- A few days later Fleur walks out of the hospital and cruises down the streets of London carrying a small suitcase. Her head pirouettes as her eyes flicker from one show poster to the next.

Caroline leans against the wall of the cabaret Burlesque. She smokes a cigarette and warms up her vocal cords. "La-la-la-la-la... Oh-oh-oh-oh-oh-ho."

Fleur halts staring at her smiling "You have a beautiful voice."

"Thanks. I'm Caroline." Extending a pack of cigarettes to Fleur.

"No, thank you. I don't smoke... but I sing. I'm Fleur."

"Really! Let's see what you've got. Come in!"

Fleur sings on stage 'Don't Give Up' a song that she composed in prison:

'Whatever life throws at me
Whatever bashes me
I'll stand up to my life

No matter what, I'll fight
Don't give up,
Please, don't give up
Oh! God I look up'
Fleur's eyes brim with tears.
'Hold on, please hold on
Spark of light in darkness, here I come
The pain is a gain in my life
The tears of wisdom
Build my kingdom
Where will is, I am
My worst enemy, sure I am
Whatever life throws at me
Whatever bashes me
I'll stand up to my life
No matter what, I'll fight
Don't give up,
Please, don't give up
Oh! God I look up'

Caroline looks at Fleur in awe and continues listening.

'Embers' dream still left in my heart
Hope is at heart
The drive is what keeps me alive
Whatever life throws at me
Whatever bashes me

I'll stand up to my life
No matter what, I'll fight
Don't give up,
Please, don't give up
Oh! God I look up'

"You have the job, girl! Where are you staying?" Asks Caroline.

"I don't know yet."

"There is a room upstairs you can have if you'd like? Deductible from your wage of course!"

"Fantastic! Thank you so much!" ---

"So that's how I met Fleur," says Caroline with tears in her eyes.

"What about my sibling? Do I have a brother or a sister?" Impatiently inquires Claire.

"Do you really want to know?

"Of course I do!"

"Well!... Eight months later..." ---

Fleur heavily pregnant sits at one of the tables with a pen in her hand, reading the L.A. Times.

Caroline joins Fleur at the table with a glass of water. "Drink! Otherwise this baby is going to thirst. What are you doing?"

"Looking for a cheap place to stay in Hollywood."

"Oh! You and your Hollywood! You are about to give birth; you can't move there with a baby. I love you like a sister, I'll help you with the child. You have a roof, a job-"

"-Yeah! But I have to go."

"Maybe not now then. It might be wiser to go when your child will be older, you will be able to leave it at nursery school while you act, sing or whatever you want to do in your Hollywood." ---

"So I convinced her to stay," Caroline mumbles bursting into tears. "I wish I didn't."

"Why?" Asks Claire.

"Because this is what happened three years later in 1988."

--- Fleur rehears on stage, "la-la-la-la. Oh-oh-oh-oh." She adjusts her microphone when three-year-old Terrance Junior, approaches her.

"Mama."

Fleur gives him a big hug and kiss. "I'm going to eat your tummy, Terry." She lifts up his shirt and starts kissing his belly repeatedly.

Terry giggles.

There is some loud circus music coming from the street.

Fleur runs to have a look at the window with Terry in her arms. "Look at the clown across the street! Let's go see him."

As Fleur walks out of the cabaret, a man in his forties, wearing a goat beard, introduces himself. "Hi! I'm Impresario Jonathan Levy."

"Fleur Larenza."

Jonathan and Fleur shake hands.

"I heard you singing last night and I really like your voice."

"Oh! Thank you."

Terry gets agitated in Fleur's arms.

"Wait sweetheart!" Fleur says to her child.

"I'm just here for a couple of days. I'm from Hollywood in California. I was wondering if you would be prepared to move. I have a contract ready for you?"

Fleur's face illuminates while her jaw drops.

Jonathan hands the contract to her. "So... Would you like to read it?"

Dazed, "Read? Of course! Oh my God! My dream! Hollywood!" Fleur puts down Terry and grabs the contract. "Stay put, baby!" She reads the piece of paper with shaking hands becoming more absorbed as she goes.

Terry walks towards the Clown.

The Clown is busy chatting with a woman on the pavement across the road.

Terry smiles hastening his pace. He gets more excited as he gets closer. Giggling, "Clown!"

A look of horror flickers across the Clown's face. His protuberant eyes flutter opened in fright as he realizes what is about to happen.

Terry's body flies like a kite in the air as he is struck by a car.

Blood sprinkles all over the Clown.

Fleur drops the contract and runs towards her inert child on the ground, "No!"

Caroline rushes out the cabaret holding Hannah in her arms.

Hannah stares at the Clown covered in blood, squeezing in her arms her pink teddy bear. ---

Claire bursts into tears interrupting Caroline, "I always wanted a sibling."

"I'm sorry. I know. It's a sad story. There is something else I need to tell you but it's enough drama for today. Let's continue another time. Shall we?"

Claire realizes that she is running late. She rushes back to her office. It's two o'clock when she arrives there. She dashes to her cubicle, but Mike catches her before she reaches it.

"You need two hours to eat your lunch?"

"Sorry Mike. I was hungry."

Gerald's head above his cubicle suddenly disappears as he lets escape a roar of laughter.

"You should be hungry for work," Mike shouts before entering his office slamming the door behind him.

Claire throws her coat on her chair and sits down holding her head in desperation.

Gerald's head appears above the cubicle, "Next time you're late bring the beast some donuts. The way to Mike's heart is through his stomach." Retreating to his cubicle smiling.

Claire takes her bottle of pills and pours a couple of them in her mouth before hiding them back in her bag. She types on her keyboard. She suddenly stops and bangs her fist on her desk "Shit!"

Gerald's head appears above the cubicle again. "Are you-"

Claire's teeth clench in anger. She points her closed fist at Gerald and unclenches it briskly, like a magical gesture that will make Gerald disappear, "-Just Pshhh."

Gerald retreats to his pigeonhole.

Mikes comes out his office and walks towards her desk," Claire!"

She is unresponsive, day dreaming hearing over and over again in her head Caroline's words, 'Terrance Junior flies like a kite in the air...' 'The bright sun rays light up the face of a screaming, blood splattered clown, with eyes popping out of his sockets...' 'Terrance Junior lies dead on the ground with his face covered in blood-'

"-Claire!"

Claire resurrects from her daydream. Baffled, "What. What?"

"I need you-"

Claire closes her eyes tousling her hair.

"-Are you fucking listening!"

"Mike. I can't concentrate!"

"I need my articles!"

Gerald comes to the rescue. He friendly taps on his boss' shoulder, "Don't worry, Mike! Claire and I are going to my place to work together on the oil spill story."

Mike brows knit as he puckers his lips.

Gerald quickly picks up a box of donuts from his desk and gives it to Mike.

Mike opens the box.

"You're going to like our perspicacious article," grabbing one of the donuts and sticking it in Mike's mouth, before he has a chance to answer. "Aren't they delicious?"

Mike, mouthful, prevails chewing like a glutton over speaking.

Gerald picks up Claire's coat and pulls her quickly towards the exit.

CHAPTER VII

Gerald's untidy apartment is modern with bright colored furniture. As he walks in, he shovels the clothes on the floor with his feet.

Trailing behind him, an amused Claire, follows his footsteps in the newly revealed path "Interesting how you're sprucing up your place."

Gerald rushes to the open kitchen. He comes back with a stained glass and a can of beer for her. He is about to pour the beverage into her cup when she interrupts him.

"Would you mind if I drink from the can?"

"No go ahead!"

She takes a sip and walks towards Gerald's big computer "Okay! Let's start working!"

Gerald grabs a chair and sit next to her.

Pearls of sweat rolls down Claire's face. She closes her eyes. Caroline's voice echoes in her head again, 'Terrance Junior flew like a kite in the air and fell down on the ground-'

"-Claire!"

She remains unresponsive.

"Claire!"

She finally opens her eyes.

Gerald strokes her face "Are you okay?"

"Yeah! I'm fine."

He moves forward and kisses her lips. The peck increases in steam.

Gerald carries her to his bedroom.

Claire giggles.

He delicately lays her on his bed where dirty pairs of underwear hang around.

Claire immediately jumps off the bed.

"What's wrong?"

"Do you have clean sheets?"

Baffled, "Clean sheets? Yeah! Wait a second!" He opens his wardrobe and grabs fresh ones that he immediately unfolds on his mattress.

They resume kissing each other.

Gerald briskly takes off all his clothes, apart from his socks.

Claire nimbly takes off all her clothes, apart from her shirt.

They both look at each other and start laughing simultaneously.

"What are you hiding under this shirt?"

Looking down "A hideous scar."

"I doubt that anything from you can be hideous. I'm pretty sure it can't be worse than my gargantuan, deformed feet."

They both laugh.

"Let's reveal on three! One. Two. Three."

Gerald pulls and kicks his socks off while Claire removes her shirt.

One of Gerald's socks ends up on her face.

They both giggle.

Gerald comes closer and strokes her scar "It's a beautiful and unique sculpture. You're one of a kind."

Claire smiles with teary eyes.

They kiss, but suddenly stop and look at one another.

"Listen! I can't do this. I have a boyfriend."

"Phew! I can't do it either."

Claire and Gerald laugh.

"I think I'm gay. Not I think. I'm gay."
Bursting into tears, shouting again "I am
gay!"

Patting his shoulder "It's okay."

Crying "It's the first time I'm saying it out
loud. I wanted so much to please my parents
that I tried to convince myself to be what they
wanted me to be. The weight of that mask is
unbearable." Shouting once more "I am gay!"
Smiling "It feels so good to be openly me."

Claire smiles looking at Gerald with envy for
his newly found freedom "I'm happy for you.
Let's get back to work now! Shall we?"

Claire returns home late that night.

She removes her coat and takes the stairs to
her bedroom. She opens her wardrobe and
hangs up her coat, when her father, knocks on
the ajar door "May I come in?"

"Hi, daddy. I thought you'd be asleep by
now."

They hug each other. He sits on her desk chair and she sits on her bed.

Terrance grabs the two golden buttons on Claire's escritoire "Who gave you the second button? Is it who I think it is?"

"Yes, papa. Fleur gave it to me before she died."

Long pause "Fleur is dead?"

"Sorry, dad. You also had a son, Terrance Junior."

"Oh my God! What! Where is he?"

"He died at three."

Terrance tousles his hair with his hands in desperation. Tears pour down his cheeks "I had no idea I had a son."

"That's what I thought." Claire nears her father and hugs him. She opens her desk drawer and takes out a file with 'Fleur Larenza' written on the cover. Claire hands it over to her father "This is what I gathered about her story so far."

Terrance opens the file and starts reading.

Lady Martha, dressed in her nightgown, stands spying behind Claire's bedroom door. She listens to their conversation. Lady Martha retires and tiptoe to the kitchen when she hears Claire saying "Terrance Junior died hit by a car while crossing the road opposite..."

Lady Martha pours some powder into two glasses on the kitchen counter.

She then slithers into Claire's bedroom carrying the tray with the beverages "Still up? What are you both talking about?"

Terrance and Claire stop their discussion.

Claire promptly snatches Fleur's file from her father's hands and puts it back in her desk drawer. Closing it "Nothing that would interest you, mother. Politics, as usual."

"Hmm! I better go back to bed then. Have something to drink." Lady Martha puts the salver on Claire's desk.

"Thank you. Good night, mommy."

She leaves her daughter's bedroom.

Later on that night, Lady Martha taps her husband's shoulder "Terrance." He is unresponsive and snoring.

Lady Martha goes on to check her daughter. Claire is sound asleep, her head on her desk "Claire." No response.

Lady Martha opens her daughter's drawer. She takes out the file 'Fleur Larenza' and reads it before putting it back.

In the middle of the night, Caroline hears a noise while she sleeps. She gets up and grabs her walking stick checking every direction inspecting each room. She sees nothing unusual, so she turns around.

Suddenly, a masked person dressed in black, grabs Caroline from behind.

"Ah!"

The intruder gags Caroline with a handkerchief, snatches her walking stick and hits her on the face and hip several times until Caroline falls on the floor.

The perpetrator then shows her a card which reads: 'Don't speak another word about Fleur Larenza or I'll kill you!'

Tears roll down Caroline's terrified eyes.

The Masked Person hits, Caroline's hip with the stick once more and shows her another card which reads: 'Do you understand?'

Caroline nods and blacks out.

The following morning, Claire on her computer at her office gets up and puts on her coat at noon time.

Gerald's head pops above the cubicle "Are you going for lunch?"

"Yes."

"Can I join you?"

"No. Sorry. I have to go somewhere."

"Can I escort you there?"

Blowing a kiss "No. See you later."

When she arrives at Caroline's place, the door is ajar "Caroline."

Caroline is terrified and tries to drag herself behind the sofa to hide.

"Oh my God! What happened?"

Caroline puts her hands on her head to protect herself.

"It's okay. It's me, Claire."

Caroline looks even more frightened.

"What happened?"

Quavering "I fell." Caroline blacks out.

When she wakes up, Claire is near her hospital bed.

Caroline looks frightened.

"Are you okay?"

Caroline nods.

"Is there anything I can do for you?"

"Go away!"

Shocked "I don't understand."

In tears "I told you everything I know about Fleur. I couldn't handle her, she disappeared from my life."

"But why don't you want to see me again?"

Upset, Caroline tries to lift her head up "Go away!"

The monitor shows that Caroline heart beats increase rapidly.

Claire gets up.

A nurse rushes in.

Claire stands in the corner next to the door looking at Caroline one more time in the eyes before she leaves.

Tears rolls down Caroline's cheeks.

Claire walks back disheartened to her office.

Mike passes by her desk "Late again! What did you eat? A whole fucking pig?" Mike retreats and slams the door behind him.

Gerald's head pops out his cubicle, laughing.

During the night, Caroline is covered in sweat and writhes in agony in her hospital bed. Out of desperation, she presses the emergency button before losing consciousness.

The doctor rushes her to the operating room.

Her hip is purple and swollen.

A surgeon is operating on her leg "We have no other choice but to amputate."

The following morning, Claire is in her office restroom. She pops some pills in her mouth before washing her hands repetitively.

In the meantime, Caroline wakes up and immediately uncovered her body. She sees her leg amputated and cries. She nervously dials numbers on the phone, atop the bedside table.

Simultaneously, the phone on Claire's desk rings non-stop.

Mike strolls by. He picks up the handset "Hello."

"I need to speak to Claire Winchester."

"I can take a message for her."

"Tell her, please, to call Caroline. It's urgent."

"Is it about the article she is writing?"

"Huh! I'm not sure... We have been talking a lot about Fleur."

Claire is back from the restroom.

"Wait a minute! Claire has returned to her desk. Let me pass you on to her."

Claire grabs the handset "Hello."

With a quivering voice "I need to talk to you. It's urgent. There is something I need to tell you."

Claire gets up, puts on her coat and dashes something off on a piece of paper before leaving her cubicle.

Mike comes face to face with her "Where are you going?"

"Hmm! I'm working on your article for the tenth anniversary of our paper."

"What is it?"

"Hmm! Something that will command front page."

Mike purses his lips, frowning "Don't dare lie to me! It's about that homeless woman. I know."

"I've got to go Mike."

"No! Don't fucking mess with me! I'm done with your crappy bullshit. If you go now you're fired."

Claire halts and struggles to make a decision "I always mess up," Claire answers before leaving.

CHAPTER VIII

Terrance looks up at the sign: '*Town Hall*'. Once inside, he looks through the alphabetic files. He picks up a folder from 1985. He nervously runs his index finger through a list of names. His finger stops at '*Fleur Larenza*,' next to her name, it's written: '*Twin Children;* '*Terrance Junior Larenza 1985-1988; Hannah Larenza 1985 adopted by Sir Terrance Winchester.*' "What the hell is that!"

In the meantime, Claire arrives at the hospital. She kisses Caroline's forehead.

Crying "I can never dance again. I might as well be dead."

"Shush! Don't say that! I saw a man with a prosthetic leg climbing a mountain on T.V. the other day."

Caroline smiles "I'm the only one left to know the truth about you."

"Truth?"

"Fleur had twins, a boy and a girl; You're Hannah, her daughter."

Claire bursts into tears reeling back in horror. She sits down on the floor grabbing her head. Mumbling "What?"

Caroline tries to reach out to her from her bed "I know it's upsetting! Shush! Stay calm!" Stroking her hair.

Claire lifts her head.

The two women stare at each other between tears.

"You have to understand what your mother went through. Let me tell you what happened after your brother's death. Don't judge her! She thought she had no other choice." ---

Caroline at Burlesque strikes numbers on the phone crying.

The phone rings at Terrance house. Lady Martha picks it up "Hello!"

"Can I speak to Terrance Winchester, please?"

"Who is it?"

Sobbing "Caroline, I'm Fleur's friend. I really need to talk to him, please."

"I would love to help, but he is not here. Can I take a message?"

"Unknown to him, Terrance is the father of Fleur's twins, Hannah and Terrance Junior... His son just died."

Pause "I'm terribly sorry to hear that. I'll pass on your message. What's your phone number?" Lady Martha jots down Caroline's number on a piece of paper.

Three days later, a Rabbi is near an open grave where Terrance junior's coffin lays.

Tears roll down Caroline's cheeks while she pats Fleur's shoulder.

Fleur in tears carries Hannah in her arms.

The little girl gives a kiss to her mother and her teddy bear.

Lady Martha is among the small gathering.

Everybody is listening to the Rabbi's Hebrew prayer:
"Yit'gadal v'yit'kadash sh'mei raba"
The congregation answers "Amen."
"b'al'ma di v'ra khir'utei
v'yam'likh mal'khutei b'chayeikhon..."

Fleur cries louder punching her own face with her fists.

Caroline in tears tries to stop her. She hugs her while Hannah stares crying at the hole where her brother's coffin is.

The Rabbi throws a handful of earth on the coffin.

Fleur lets herself fall on her knees screaming in tears. She violently scratches her own face until it bleeds "My little baby boy! Mommy is coming too."

Caroline crouches down and holds Fleur in her arms kissing her head "Please, stop doing that."

"I want to die to! Oh God! How much more can one be stricken by? Please! I can't take no more. I give up. I give up. I... Give... Uuup!"

Hannah walks to the hole and throws her pink teddy bear atop her brother's coffin. ---

Claire's face floods in tears, sinking more and more into desperation.

--- After the funeral, Fleur slouches in a chair at a table, drinking a bottle of wine in the deserted cabaret.

Hannah sits on the ground at her mother's feet.

Lady Martha enters the room. She approaches the little girl and squats down stroking her hair. She gives her a doll in a little white dress "Hi! It's for you. You are so adorable."

Lady Martha stands up and sits down on a chair next to Fleur "I'm terribly sorry that Terrance is not here with me. He thought that it would be inappropriate to see you again."

Fleur fires back a furious look at her.

"I'm on your side and I believe he should have come in person to sort his own business. Hannah is beautiful. I always wanted a girl. Unfortunately, I cannot have any children. Listen! Terrance and I, have the means to give Hannah a wonderful life-"

"-Get out! I can't believe you came here intending to take my daughter! Get out!"

Lady Martha gets up "Terrance wants his daughter! He is scared she'll end up like her brother in your care."

An enraged Fleur impetuously grabs the empty bottle on the table but refrains her instinct to strike.

Lady Martha leaves the room briskly.

Fleur bursts into tears and strikes the bottle on the table. She slices her wrist with the bottleneck. She slowly falls down into a pool of blood. Her eyelids flicker open staring at her crying daughter.

Hannah drops the doll in the puddle "Mama."

A tear rolls down Fleur's cheek before she falls unconscious.

Caroline finds her on the floor and dials 999.

Caroline embraces Fleur's body as the paramedic walks in. She promptly grabs the bottle neck and hides it behind her back.

Two Paramedics put Fleur on a stretcher.

"How did she do that?" Asks one of them.

Stroking Hannah's head "She slipped with the bottle in her hand and fell on it," answers Caroline.

On their way out, their feet kick on the now bloody crimson doll.

Fleur is asleep on a hospital bed.

Caroline is by her bedside in a chair playing climbing spider with Hannah on her lap "The spider is climbing your arm all the way up to your neck." She tickles the child's neck.

Hannah giggles.

Fleur opens her eyes and smiles.

Lady Martha enters the room with a flower bouquet.

Caroline frowns "I think you should leave."

"I'm profusely sorry, Fleur. I'm here to help. Please! Listen to what I have to say."

Fleur nods.

"Hannah! Let's get some candies while mommy talk to the lady!" Caroline leaves the room with the little girl.

After a long discussion, Fleur signs some papers.

Caroline comes back with Hannah. Caroline strokes Fleur's hair "Are you sure it's what you want?"

Fleur nods in tears.

Lady Martha pulls Hannah by her hand "Come on, pretty girl! Let's get some more candies."

Hannah cooperates "Yeah! I love candies." She turns around looking at her mom "Mama."

Fleur burst into tears.

Hannah starts crying and tries pulling away from Lady Martha's grip screaming "Mama!"

Lady Martha pulls Hannah briskly outside.

Caroline and Fleur's faces are flooded in tears wringing each other hands.

"Are you sure you can trust her?" Inquires Caroline.

"I trust Terrance. I want Hannah to be happy and have a better life." ---

In Tears "Oh my God! Dad didn't know Fleur was pregnant. He had no clue she had children," interrupts Claire before rushing towards the door.

Caroline looks at her baffled and tormented.

Claire leaves the room slamming the door. She exits the hospital and runs down the narrow alleys like a bird who has just been released from his coop. A sudden gust of rain lashes her face as she runs frantically in tears down the street. Out of breath, Claire halts and punches repeatedly a tree in Hyde Park. Blood oozes from her hands. She leans her back against the trunk letting herself sag slowly in desperation until her behind anchors in a quagmire. She convulsively fidgets her feet. After hesitation, fighting her fear of germs, Claire plunges her two hands in the mud crying. She then rubs them on her face before getting up. She wanders aimlessly and despondently through the park, soaked, dragging her feet like a zombie. Her handbag slides off her lifeless dangling arm scattering its content on the ground. The rain swamps James' picture. Claire kneels down and grabs the photo hugging it against her heart crying. She picks up her drenched cellphone hitting numbers. It's not working. In a rage she smashes it on the ground "Ah!" She stands up and starts running. She is getting closer to the park's exit and James' building. She smiles and starts running towards it, opening her arms as if she wants to embrace it. Claire slowly decrescendos her steps as she strains her eyes peering through the blur curtain of pearled rain enwrapping two familiar silhouettes.

James opens an umbrella mirroring a smile to Lisa.

Claire halts a distance away from the building and wipes her eyes in disbelief.

James and her close friend kiss each other passionately.

Numbness overwhelms Claire's eyes before closing them as she screams in chorus with booming thunder in the sky "Ha!" Claire bites her lip, writhing in suppressed fury, hiding by stooping down behind a parked truck. Her body squirms in an emotional agony as she burst into tears.

She slouches on a bench facing a pond looking at the rainbow. She pops some pills in her mouth before drinking a bottle of wine staggering towards a Duck with a red bill.

To the duck "Hey buddy! Have some wine!"

The Duck runs away and Claire chases it.

Claire falls on the ground.

The Duck stops running.

"Why are you swaying your butt like that? I'm done with men so don't try to seduce me, buddy!"

A mother with her young daughter stroll by.

The little girl feeds the Duck with a big chunk of bread.

Claire frowns. Slurring "Hey! It's my buddy, not yours!"

The frightened little girl hurries back to her mom "Mummy!"

The mother grabs her daughter's hand and retreats.

Claire shouts to their back "How do you know she is really your mom?" Claire crawls to the duck who runs away leaving the bread on the ground. Claire grasps the morsel. She tears a small piece and pours some wine into it before offering it to the duck "Here, buddy, have this!"

The Duck comes towards her, snatches the piece with its red bill before waddling back.

"Ha! Ha! With a nose like that I knew you were a boozer!" Claire pours some wine into another piece of bread.

It's getting dark. Claire and the Duck still stagger side by side.

She takes a sip of beer "Buddy, would you like some?" Claire crouches pouring a fountain of the ale. The Duck happily drinks.

A Man creeps behind, clutches and assaults her.

Claire grovels as the assailant hauls her by her feet towards a secluded area in the wood.

"Ah! Help!"

He flips Claire and slaps her across the face.

She retaliates kicking and wriggling but the Man pins her down firmly before pulling her trousers down.

"No! Please! No!"

The Man gags her.

The Duck comes close to Claire, quacking.

The bushwacker hits the strident noisy Duck.

The blow propels the bird outside the wooded area.

Two homeless men and Bella, walking by, look in the direction of the Duck.

The two homeless men rush to Claire's rescue.

Claire wrenches herself free of her attacker's grip.

The aggressor runs away.

Claire huddles in tears.

Bella strokes Claire's hair "What are you doing here all alone at this time? It's dangerous in here. Come with us!"

The three homeless people and Claire walk away followed by the Duck.

They finally join other roofless vagabonds around a fire-barrel under a bridge. The majority of them either drink or shoot up while others lay on cardboard beds with newspaper blankets.

Claire drinks some beer while giggling with them "How did you all end up here?"

"I used to have a decent job at the supermarket. My mother got sick and needed an operation to remove a tumor. She was on a N.H.S. waiting list and was getting worst. I used all my saving for her medications, then I lost my job because I had to look after her. My mother died because of that fucking N.H.S. waiting list," Bella responds before injecting her arm with heroin."

"Hey! Don't use it all, I need some too!" Interrupts a Red Haired Woman. "Me, I left Ireland for a better life until my unbearable hunger got quenched by a pimp with a big hotdog."

A Toothless Man joins the conversation "I was a receptionist in a big hotel. I had an accident and broke my front teeth. I got fired because my smile scared the clients. I couldn't afford a dentist. Then my wife ran off with another man. I lost everything. I have no dreams, no life to look forward to."

Bella dribbles and slurs as she speaks with half opened eyes to the Duck "And you, Ducky, how did you end up here?"

Everybody laughs.

"The Duck is an addict too. And I'm his dealer," proudly shouts Claire.

"And what about you?" Questions the Irish babe to Claire.

"Me?" Claire's smile, leaps from happiness to wistfulness gazing through her surrounded fellow vagabonds abasing themselves in various destructive and self-degrading ways "Who knows!"

The following morning, Claire wakes pushing away her newspaper blanket looking at the rose pink light of dawn. She notices Bella's purple face with dry blood on her mouth. Claire walks near her "Bella." Giving her a shake, "Bella!" Claire holds Bella's wrist "Shit! Someone call an ambulance, please!"

Claire and the other homeless people watch the ambulance drive away.

Claire takes out her bottle of pills from her pocket and looks at it pensively. She peeks one more time at the disappearing ambulance. She deeply breathes in and out before opening the bottle and throws all her pills in the trash. Tears of relief wash her face. As Claire walks away, she takes out her last can of beer. She opens it and pour its content along her footpath on the ground as she walks with a smile on her face.

The duck flies away.

Claire jumps and throws her arms in the air. "Freedom!"

CHAPTER IX

Claire is back in her home. She resembles a scarecrow with mud stained clothes and entangled scruffy ringlet hair. She climbs up the stairs with a haggard look.

At the same time she reaches the last step, Lady Martha comes out of her bedroom. The unpleasant face to face happenstance frightened her mother "Ah!"

Claire's frowzy frame shakes with mirth of delight.

Lady Martha strains her eyes in disbelief as she takes a more scrutinized double take at her offspring "Oh my God! Claire."

Staring defiantly at her antagonist "Nope. I am Hannah."

A look of horror flickers across Lady Martha's winced face "What!... What?... What happened to your clothes?"

Claire forcibly pulls out her own cashmere sweater through her neck and tears it apart, exposing her bare disfigured chest "Do I look more like my real mom now?"

"Have you lost your mind?"

Claire picks a booger from her nose and eats it.

"Huh! Are you mad? I don't recognize you."

"So be it! I'm mad. What about you? Who are you?"

"Don't be ridiculous! You know who I am."

"Yeah! You're a fraud!"

"Claire-"

"-Hannah! I'm Hannah the proud daughter of Fleur Larenza." Burps.

"Oh God! Listen, I don't know what this is all about but you are my daughter." Lady Martha comes closer and holds her.

Claire wriggles free, moves swiftly away and gives Lady Martha a peevish frown.

"Listen-"

"-Are you going to deliver one of your breathless and effortless spiels promoting your bullshit?"

"Oh, please! Watch your language."

"Come on! Reel off your shit!"

"I-"

"-Sorry, but I have no time for your lies."

Terrance enters his house, and walks up the stairs. "Neither do I!" Throwing a document in his wife's face "This paper says I adopted Hannah Larenza. Where is my daughter?"

"Dad. I'm Hannah."

"No. You are not!" Answer in chorus Lady Martha and Terrance.

"Martha! Where is Hannah?"

"Leave me alone!"

Terrance walks aggressively towards his wife, grabbing her by her neck. He squeezes.

"Daddy. Let go!"

Terrance removes his hands.

Lady Martha immediately moves away. She loses her balance and falls. Her body tumbles down the stairs and hit the corner of a marble coffee table.

Claire and Terrance rush down to her.

Blood comes out of Lady Martha's mouth and head.

Crying "Mommy."

Lady Martha opens her eyes.

"We need to call an ambulance," Terrance to his daughter.

Quavering "I'm sorry for the pain I caused you both. You want the truth; I'll give it to you. I'm not proud of it."

--- 1988, soon after Lady Martha left Fleur's hospital bed with little Hannah.

A Stewardess passes by them offering drinks on a trolley "What would you like to drink?"

"A Scotch, please," answer Lady Martha. "What would you like to drink, Hannah?"

"Nothing."

The Stewardess serves Lady Martha her drink.

Hannah is in a grumpy mood "Where are we going?"

"To Russia, the land of Santa Claus."

Hannah's eyes glint for a moment before frowning in discontentment "When will I see mummy?"

"Santa Claus will give you all the toys you want and you can ask him a big present for your mom. She will be so happy when you'll give it to her."

Hannah's face illuminates with joy.

Their driver stops at a mansion somewhere in the Russian countryside. It's snowing heavily. Hannah and Lady Martha step out the car.

They walk towards the house.

"Is this where Santa Claus lives?" Asks Hannah.

"Yes it is."

"I'm going to ask him for a lot of presents for mummy. I don't want anything for myself. I just want my mother to be well and happy."

Hannah sits in an armchair next to a fireplace.

A Doctor with a syringe approaches the little girl.

Lady Martha lifts up Hannah's sleeve "Be a good girl! The doctor is going to take some of your blood."

Hannah cries retracting her arm "No! I don't like needles!"

"Listen! We need to take some drops of your blood for Santa Claus. He is going to make a magical potion for your mom with it. Don't you want your mummy to be better?"

Hannah wipes her tears with her hand and nods courageously giving her arm to the doctor showing her true mettle. The little girl closes her eyes facing the other direction while the doctor draws her blood.

The following morning, Hannah walks in the dining room where her breakfast waits for her on the table with a present wrapped next to it.

"You see Santa Claus left you a present and after breakfast he is going to give you many more," Lady Martha says.

Hannah smiles and grabs the present. As the child unveils the wrapping paper, a clown puppet appears. Hannah's facial expressions darken. She screams incessantly holding her head dropping the clown on the floor. Hannah's voice becomes increasingly sharp, almost strident "Aaaaah!"

Lady Martha gives her a drink "Shush! Drink that!" Forcibly pouring the beverage in the little girl's mouth.

Hannah's vision immediately becomes blurred and she hears in slow motion the Doctor's steps entering the room.

"So?" Lady Martha anxiously asks him.

"She is a match!"

Hannah collapses on the floor. She stares at the clown before closing her teary eyes completely.

They carry the little girl to an operating table.

The surgeon starts cutting her chest.

The heart rate monitor shows strong beats that stop abruptly when the doctor extracts Hannah's heart.

After the operation, Lady Martha is on the phone with Terrance "How is Claire doing?" She asked her husband.

Terrance looks distraught and exhausted "Not well. The doctor said she has only a couple of weeks to live."

"I have great news. A Russian girl has just died in a car crash and her heart is a perfect match." ---

Claire and Terrance are in tears.

Lady Martha stare at them.

"You are a monster," screams Terrance.

"No! I'm a loving mother that did everything in her power to save her child's life," responds Lady Martha before her last breath.

He checks her pulse. Nothing.

Terrance and Claire look at each other horrified.

When the paramedics arrive, a policeman questions them "What happened?"

"I-"

Claire interrupts her father "-She was about to go down the stairs when I called her. She turned around, lost her balance and fell down the stairs."

Terrance and her daughter look at each other in tears.

The following morning, Claire walks on the sidewalk and stops abruptly when a child passes next to her holding a clown face birthday balloon. To self, holding her heart "It's okay." Claire inhales, exhales and smiles as she has overcome her heart's fear of clowns. Claire's phone rings. She picks it up. It's James "Get lost!"

James drives speaking on his cell phone. Shocked "What! What's wrong?"

"I have to go. I don't want to waste one more minute of my precious saliva with a scumbag like you."

"Claire-"

Claire hangs up.

James looks flabbergasted. He dials in disbelief her number again.

Claire's phone rings. Claire presses the button 'ignore'. She passes by a storefront with a mirror. She stops and looks at her reflection smiling giving herself the thumb up. To self "I'm proud of you!" Pointing her index finger at her reflection "Respect."

Claire enters an Italian restaurant, to meet Gerald.

"Finally! I get to have lunch with you!

Laughter.

I'm sorry about your mom."

"Thank you. It's OK." Claire gives him a file "Please give that to Mike for me."

Gerald holds her hand across the table "I'm worried about you, Claire."

"You shouldn't. I threw the mask away too. The journey was long and painful but I finally found happiness. I'm now following my intrinsic drive. I am going to be what I was born to be."

The following day, Mike sits at his desk when Claire enters.

Her ex-boss gets up ecstatically and shakes hands with her.

"Congratulation on your article. It's a big hit!" He grabs a newspaper and gives it to Claire.

On the front page it's written: '*The Homeless Victims of The N.H.S. Waiting List.*'

Claire smiles.

"Sorry for firing you. The political editor position is yours."

"Thank you Mike but... I have to decline."

Taken by surprise "Decline? Why Claire?"

"I want to create a newspaper called: 'Intrinsic'. I will write stories about people who had a dream and made it a reality. The profit will help others who gave up on theirs, like the homeless and individuals that want to kill themselves. Hopefully, I can help some to get back on track and discover hope for them to pursue what is essential to their soul finding true happiness."

"Soul?"

"Yes. Happiness evolves around five needs: Food. A roof. Safety. Health. And the most important, the healing of the soul."

"The healing of the soul? Hum... To me, food is my sole healing".

"Why do you think that more and more well off teenagers commit suicide? They lack the fifth need. Life is like sailing a boat. You have to go through the torrid waves whenever they come at you. But if you're not equipped with those five needs, believe me you'll sink. Making peace with the real you by being who you truly are is paramount to the healing of your soul."

Mike looks confused "Sounds profound... Well! Good luck, Claire!"

Before leaving Mike's office, Claire quickly throws a few more words "Oh! By the way, I want to be called Hannah from now on."

"OK! Hannah the philosopher!" Laughter.

Few days later, Claire holds a jar containing Fleur's ashes.

Terrance sits next to her in a helicopter above the Hollywood sign in California.

Claire opens the lid of the jar.

She and her father's eyes brim with tears.

From the cockpit, Claire scatters Fleur's ashes over the Hollywood Sign "You finally made it."

"I will always love you, Fleur. Rest in peace my beautiful star," adds Terrance.

Claire opens a carton box that belonged to Fleur. There is a picture of Hannah and Terrance Junior. There is also the twenty pounds note stained with red ink that Claire gave her. Claire burst into tears when she sees that Fleur drew a heart with the written name of Hannah in the middle of it.

Terrance holds his daughter and looks at the picture, "Hannah looked exactly like you as a child."

Terrance and Claire look at each other with a smile.

Later that evening, Terrance and Claire walk back to their hotel.

They stop in front of a giant street poster. The picture is divided in three horizontal frames. The first one is in black and white, showing American slaves juxtaposed with Jewish slaves from the time of pharaoh. The middle part is sepia, showing Martin Luther King. The third part, in vibrant colors, has three people holding a single torch together. Among them, Nelson Mandela, Chaim Azriel Weizmann and a woman holding proudly a voting ballot in her other hand.

Across the poster it's written: '*Some dreams are abandoned, while others are crushed, but as long as embers remain, the relay can be passed on until someone makes it real.*'

"What's your dream dad?"

"My dream? I don't know."

"Look deep down inside you. What inner passions have come to you instinctively?"

Thinking "Oh! Yes. I always wanted to go around the world in my biplane."

"Go for it dad. It's never too late. Never give up on your dream."

THE END